In the Night Garden

Barbara Joosse

illustrated by Elizabeth Sayles

Henry Holt and Company

New York

For Florita, mother of my heart—B. J.

For Matt & Jessie, as always

Special thanks to three little girls:
Louise, Phoebe, and Amara—E. S.

Henry Holt and Company, LLC
Publishers since 1866
175 Fifth Avenue
New York, New York 10010
www.HenryHoltKids.com

Henry Holt® is a registered trademark of Henry Holt and Company, LLC.
Text copyright © 2008 by Barbara Joosse
Illustrations copyright © 2008 by Elizabeth Sayles
All rights reserved.
Distributed in Canada by H. B. Fenn and Company Ltd.

Library of Congress Cataloging-in-Publication Data
Joosse, Barbara M.
In the night garden / by Barbara Joosse ; illustrated by Elizabeth Sayles.—1st ed.
p.   cm.
Summary: Three friends play in a garden before bedtime, each one imagining
herself a different animal.
ISBN-13: 978-0-8050-6671-5 / ISBN-10: 0-8050-6671-3
[1. Imagination—Fiction. 2. Night—Fiction. 3. Animals—Fiction. 4. Play—Fiction.]
I. Sayles, Elizabeth, ill. II. Title.
PZ7.J7435In 2008   [E]—dc22   2007002824

First Edition—2008
The artist used acrylic paints and pastels on paper to create the illustrations for this book.
Printed in China on acid-free paper. ∞

10 9 8 7 6 5 4 3 2 1

Three little girls prowl the night garden.

Rrrrrrr

One is a bear
with sharp, white teeth.
She tears berries from the branches,
slurping and smacking,
licking her lips.
Rrrrrrr, the bear rumbles.
Mmmmmm, the bear smacks.

Mmmmm

One is a whale,
gargantuan.
She cruises dark water,
low and slow,
moaning a song to the silvery moon.
Eeee-eeee-eeee! sings the whale.

Eeee-eeee-eeee

How-how-howl

One is a sled dog,
sleek and lean.
She runs with the pack,
then throws back her head
and *how-how-howls*
to the deep dark sky.

Danger!

The bear growls a warning.
The whale dives deep.
The dog sniffs the air.

Eeeee

No! No!
Rraaaaowr! roars the bear.
Haaoooo! howls the dog.
Eeeee! cries the whale.

Bedtime!

One little girl rolling in the water—
spraying through her blowhole,
whooshing and splashing,
swimming the sea.

One little girl slipping on her bearskin—
arms in the arm holes,
legs in the leg holes,
fuzzy and soft.

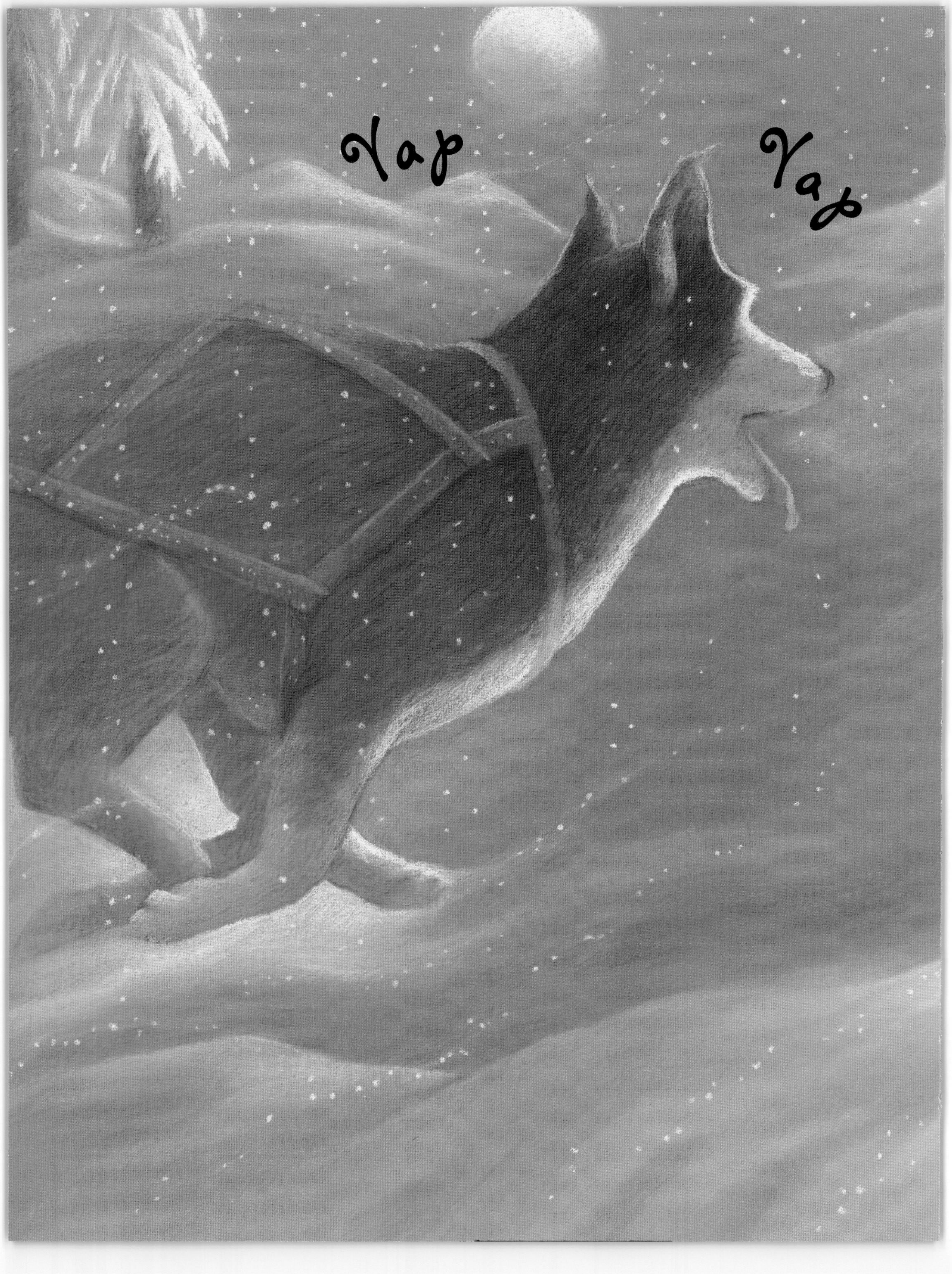
Yap
Yap

Yap

One little girl pulling a dogsled—
lapping and yapping,
frosty in the moonlight,
riding and gliding on feathery snow.

$\mathcal{T}$hree little girls, r

One dives,
one crawls,
one curls beneath the covers.
Ahhh.

Ahhh

$\mathcal{N}$ow
three little girls close their eyes
and open their dreams.

They prowl the dream garden,
singing
and growling
and howling to the deep
dark
sky.

Good night.